KNOCKOUT

KNOCKOUT

A 12:01 NOVELLA

MONTREZ

KNOCKOUT

This is a work of fiction. Names, characters, places, and incidents either are the product of the author's imagination or are used fictitiously. Any resemblance to actual persons, living or dead, events, or locales is entirely coincidental.

Knockout (A 12:01 Trilogy Novella)
© 2020 by Montrez

Cover Design by Raw Design Studios
Editing by Make Your Mark Publishing Solutions
Interior Design by Make Your Mark Publishing Solutions

Published by Novel Creatures Publications
Columbus, OH

Printed in the United States of America
First Edition, September 2020

Paperback ISBN: 978-1-7347670-2-5
eBook ISBN: 978-1-7347670-3-2
+

For you,
Dear Reader

PREFACE

HEALING IS THE WORST KIND OF PAIN. Resetting broken bones. Righting dislocated limbs and jammed appendages. It's painful, and it's ugly. Scars line the surface of my skin, visible beacons of old wounds I'll never be able to completely erase. Sometimes I count the marks the way some people count their blessings. Every scar is a mark of survival, not failure. Strength, not weakness. At least that's what I tell myself when I get scared. And there's nothing scarier than what I'm facing now.

Forget that a bunch of homicidal, immortal hunters want to kill me. Forget about the fact that they've almost succeeded in wiping out so many others like me. I'm an Errant, armed with agility, strength, and killer reflexes, but the odds are stacked against us. With everything we can do, Errants are no match for our unkillable enemy. They have unlimited resources and thousands of years of knowledge between them. We're fighting a losing war.

There's so much I could be worrying about right now. But I'm worried about a girl. I haven't known Savannah long. I don't know when or how she managed to burrow under my calloused skin, but I can't shake the way I feel about her or the way I want her to feel about me.

Savannah sits next to me on the sidewalk.

"Everyone else is knocked out. Aren't you exhausted after everything that's happened?"

Tonight was hard. We lost a lot of friends. We almost lost our own lives, but it's nothing new. I've been fighting impossible battles even before the Immortals started hunting me. I stood up for myself once, and that one triumph turned into a never-ending nightmare.

I thought it would end the fighting, but I was wrong.

There's a world hidden in the folds of everyday life. I slipped through those cracks, and though I've fought with everything in me to escape, I keep getting pulled back down. I've been drafted into a war I never knew existed, a fight that challenges everything I thought I knew. Monsters exist, but they aren't hideous beasts hiding in the closets or under beds. They hide behind humans, twisted by ambition, driven by thirst for power and control.

The corners of Savannah's mouth twitch with a nervous grin, pulling me out of my thoughts.

"Do you want me to call you K.O. or Oliver?"

I frown. No one's ever asked me what I wanted to be called. Everyone just calls me K.O.

Savannah bites her lip. "I thought you might like K.O. better. Because of her. Doc says there was a girl who gave you the nickname."

Her tone is soft but prodding. She hugs

her legs and rests her chin on her knees, waiting for me to answer the question she hasn't asked. When the silence between us continues, her eyes narrow, and she studies my face.

"I like Oliver."

Me too, I want to say, but the words won't come out.

Her cheeks redden, and she looks away from me. "They say you get in these moods and disappear for a while. Where do you go?"

Savannah's the least self-aware person I know—self-deprecating and unsure—but when she looks at me, I feel naked even though I'm fully dressed. It's like she can see all my scars, every imperfection, right down to the cracks in the mask I try to wear. She's always curious, and she isn't afraid to question everything. She's a breath of air so fresh, she takes my breath away.

She frowns at me. Her awkward shyness dissolves with her irritation. "This brooding, mysterious thing has to go. If we're going to stand a chance against the Immortals, we have to learn to trust each other. You practically know my whole life story. I don't know anything about you. I feel like I'm the only one walking around in the dark."

I wipe my sweaty hands on my jeans. "We're all walking around in the dark, if you ask me."

Her eyes soften. "You sure make it look easy."

I snort. Maybe she's not as observant as I thought. She sees me, but she doesn't get me. I'm afraid what will happen when she finally does.

She scoots closer to me and shifts to rest her head on my shoulder. Her wild hair is soft against my skin. She emits a comforting warmth. It puts me at ease, more than I want to admit. We sit still and quiet for so long, I wonder if she's asleep, but then she lifts her head to look at me.

"You know, you don't have to walk in the dark alone. Not anymore."

I can handle anger, disappointment, fighting, and even being ignored, but the soft expectation in her eyes unnerves me. Part of me wants to push her away and run before I crumble, but I can't move. Part of me doesn't want to.

I draw in a breath. "What do you want to know?"

CHAPTER ONE

FIGHT OR DIE. IT'S THE MOST IMPORTANT rule around here. My strained muscles scream for me to quit, but I can't stop fighting. I welcome the pain. It keeps me focused. It keeps me alive. I'm not ready to die.

I ignore the hunger gnawing at my insides. My scalp tingles. I shake off the numbness and narrow my eyes in focus. I block out the rowdy crowds and their bold bets. My opponent is twice my age, three times my weight. His bulging muscles promise strength, but his size is also his weakness. He may be larger than me, but I'm quick on my feet. All I have to do is dodge the right punches and evade the right holds long enough.

"Scared, kid?" he asks.

I raise my fists. "Hungry."

He blinks. I swing, hitting him in the jaw. The contact has little impact. The man grunts, spits, and swings back. I duck, nearly crumpling to the ground. My ribs are still raw and sore from the last beating. Inhaling, I pull myself up and find my back against the cage. There's no running from this fight. There's no running from any fight, but when I'm finished with the steroid giant, he'll wish he *had* run.

His hands reach out to grip both sides of my head. I slip out of his hold just as his knee rises, striking me in the chin and nose. My neck jerks back. Pain builds. Adrenaline spikes. Instinct kicks in. My fists tighten. My opponent charges at me, reaching for me a second time. I sidestep at the last minute. He stumbles forward and crashes into the cage. I kick him in the back of his knee while he's vulnerable. His leg buckles. I put him in the strongest chokehold I can as he struggles to catch his balance. He headbutts me from behind, hitting me in the nose again. I fall back from the impact and scramble to my feet as he turns to glare at me.

"I'ma tear your head off!"

He's angry, but his leg is dragging. I look to the only familiar face watching from the crowd. I'm offered a small, impassive nod. I race to the other side of the cage. The crowd boos. I block out the noise as my opponent ambles forward. Pushing my back into the cage, I breathe deep before propelling forward. I've survived a lot of fights, but the fear never goes away. I embrace that fear. I harness it. My frantic heartbeat, my heightened instinctive awareness, the numbing panic, the anger … I use it all to fuel the strength swelling within me. Adrenaline kicks into overdrive, electrifying every nerve and muscle, blocking everything but an overwhelming sense of power. My fist meets flesh, and the impact sounds like thunder, echoing through the entire Colosseum. The whites of my opponent's eyes show as his head snaps back. His body flies and crashes into the mat.

Shock silences the crowd. The cage opens. I'm escorted out of the ring and out of the pit as obscenities erupt. No one expected the slim Korean boy to knock out the Marine even though the fight plays out the same every night.

"The fight's rigged," a man screams above the rest of the chaos.

I stop, training my stare on the man.

"I'll knock those pretty teeth out your mouth!" he snarls.

I turn back to the cage. Food will have to wait. The heckler presses his way eagerly through the crowd, taking his shirt off to showcase flabby muscle. After the last fight, I know I don't have time to waste on theatrics. Pain, hunger, and thirst can only motivate me so far before my body shuts down. The man dances on his toes, throwing insults instead of fists. I don't need to build momentum. The last bit of strength clings to me like static, and

I unleash it in a forceful wave. My fist hits his mouth. There's a sickening crunch, and his body smacks against the floor. He cries out and clutches his bloody mouth. I walk past the heap of a man as he kneels, trembling, looking for cracked pieces of his teeth.

"Cracked ribs. Nose sprain. Jammed index and middle finger and a possible concussion," Dr. Holden says.

Roman frowns, his disapproval one of the only expressions he allows to cross his severe face. "When can he fight again?"

Dr. Holden hesitates under the pressure of Roman's gaze. "Safely? With the possibility of a concussion, two weeks. At least give him a few days' rest."

With a huge meal, some narcotics, and medicine-induced sleep, I'll probably be back in the cage in two days tops.

"You won. You eat," Roman says.

Hunger is the most painful sensation after

a fight. Every other ache is dull in comparison. Fight or die is the most important rule. Win or starve is the second. Other fighters aren't as fortunate as me. Some guys don't always win their fights. Some don't make it out the ring. There are guys who haven't eaten in weeks, and because of it, their chance of surviving our training and cage matches is slim. I slip them food when I can.

"Could everyone eat this time?" I ask.

Hunger hits me harder tonight than it has in a while. I don't know if I'll have the strength or discipline to deny myself a sufficient helping. Splitting meals doesn't really help anyone.

"You know the rules," Roman reminds me.

I don't speak. Instead, I hold my breath, waiting for his answer. I try to match the stoic look Roman gives me, hoping my fear doesn't show. I know I'm pushing my luck. Trying to help the other boys might do more harm than good, but it's hard to eat knowing everyone else is starving.

Roman nods. It's a slight, barely perceivable

motion, but it's more than enough for me. Tentative relief washes over me, soothing the tension until only hunger and exhaustion remain.

"Tomorrow, you will fight for them. If you remain undefeated, everyone eats. Fail me in any way, and you'll all starve. Do you understand?"

Dr. Holden's eyes widen in objection, but he keeps silent, his lips forming a tight, narrow line. I ignore him, nodding at Roman.

Roman strides out of the room, leaving the doctor to finish tending to my injuries.

The gray-haired man wraps my hand in gauze, jerking the fabric tightly around. I frown at him. He glares at me.

"What are you thinking? You're going to get yourself killed!"

I grimace. "It's not the worst thing that could happen."

He grabs my shirt and pulls me closer to whisper, "Those boys will never survive if you fight all their battles, and neither will you."

I don't want to fight all their battles. "I just wanted to give them a fighting chance."

"You're just a kid yourself!" he says. The passion in his voice causes him to spit in my face.

I flinch more at his words than anything, but I wipe the spit off my face with the back of my hand. "Are you done?"

Dr. Holden shakes his head, but he backs down. "At least take the painkillers."

He shakes a few white pills from a medicine bottle and offers them to me. I shake my head.

He growls. "Stubborn boy!"

I hold back a smile. Giving Dr. Holden a hard time is the only fun I can look forward to these days, but I try not to push too much. The old man cares about me as much as someone in his line of work can. If it wasn't for him, I'd probably be dead by now.

"Fine."

His face softens just a little. He offers me the pills with a bottle of ice-cold water.

"I'll prepare some ointments and some

things for you to take before tomorrow's fights. It should give you an edge."

I'll need more than an edge. I'll need a miracle.

CHAPTER TWO

I WAS TEN WHEN I WAS TAKEN. IT WAS A SIM-ple grocery store trip gone wrong. I offered to put the cart away while Mom packed the groceries in the trunk. I never made it back. Sometimes I lay awake on my hard mattress wondering how long it took her to realize I was gone. I wonder how long she searched the parking lot and the store. What happened when Dad found out I was gone?

It's been four years since then. I doubt they're still looking, but sometimes I wonder if they still think about me the way I think of them. I try not to imagine what life is like for them now. Instead, I hold onto the memories we had. Remembering Mom's cooking comforts me when hunger gets to be too much. Dad's old goofy jokes are like medicine when the painkillers don't fully kick in, and remembering their smiles keeps me human in a world that's trying to turn me into a monster.

I tell myself I'm doing the right thing, that my parents would be proud of me. They taught me to do what was right, not what was easy. As hard as life gets living at the Colosseum, I'd like to think I can still recognize the difference, and gorging on food and tossing scraps at starving human beings just isn't right.

"Oliver," a quiet voice prods against the dark.

My throat tightens when he says my name, but we all have an unspoken agreement to use one another's given names as much as possible. It helps us hold onto who we were before the Colosseum.

"Yeah, Nolan?" I say, shifting uncomfortably in bed, trying to ignore my still-raging hunger.

"Thanks for the food."

I ate as little as I could tonight, and Dr. Holden, an accomplice in my small, vain rebellion, spread the rest to the other boys.

Someone vomits, the food too heavy for their stomach. Soup. Tomorrow, I'll ask for soup or broth. Something. Anything to help them.

"It's Emery. Don't think he's gonna make it much longer," Nolan says.

He probably won't, and if I fail tomorrow, none of us will.

※

The weight of my body presses against the hard mattress. I feel heavy, but my head is light. Just as I slide into sleep, a loud crash jolts me into half-awareness. Instinct overrides delirium. I sit up too fast, and the room spins. I clutch the side of my bed to steady myself.

Nolan's voice cuts through the sudden chaos. "New guy's up. Sedatives must've worn off."

Shame. The painkillers are just starting to work on me, and I really needed that sleep.

"Save your energy. You're not getting out of here!" I want to yell.

Instead, I grind down on my teeth and will myself to sleep. The pain and the background noise dull as darkness swallows me into peaceful unconsciousness. But peace never lasts. I wake up to stiff, swollen joints and a pounding headache. Pain agitates every nerve in my body, and my stomach twists in agonizing waves of nausea. I roll on my side and fold my legs with my knees to my chest, as if curling into a fetal position will somehow bring relief.

The door to my quarters opens after several of the locks are undone. Dim, yellow light blinks on and off before casting a steady, weak florescent glow. I force myself to push the pain to the back of my mind, preparing for what I'll have to face. Roman strides into the room, straightening his suit. I scramble to my feet, gritting my teeth to bear the pain of the movement. Roman grunts, the closest sound I've ever heard to a laugh. He motions for me to sit. I hesitate, but pain floods my senses, almost knocking the oxygen out of me. I stumble backward, falling onto my bed.

Roman doesn't miss a thing, especially when it comes to weakness. He studies me for a long moment, and when he speaks, his words are careful.

"You are not as obedient as you pretend to be. I know all about what you and the doctor do."

I stare at my hands as if that's enough to will them to stop shaking.

"It was my idea. I'm sorry. I—"

He raises a hand to interrupt me. I flinch, expecting something else. It won't be the first or last time I've been reprimanded.

Instead, the corner of his mouth twitches. "You're still afraid of me. Good."

I'll never admit it out loud, but I have several reasons to be afraid of Roman. Those reasons are etched in my skin, ghosts of scars that will never fully heal. When I first arrived at his compound, I stubbornly fought to escape. It was a hard, painful lesson, but Roman made his point clear. The Colosseum, as he called it, was my home.

He flicks his hand, just a slight motion, but the command is clear. Dr. Holden scurries into my room. He hands me a handful of pills and a disposable cup of cool water. His hands shake as bad as mine, and he almost spills the water in my lap. His face is swollen, bruised, covered with sweat and dried blood. Sniffing, he wipes his nose with the back of his hand before preparing and working a thick salve of smelly ointments on my hands, arms, and legs. He doesn't speak or spare me a glance. He has as much reason to be afraid of Roman as any of us. His fresh wounds are evidence of that. When the doctor finishes checking and tending to my injuries, he excuses himself with no hint of lingering consideration. I know this is the last time I can count on him to help beyond what's expected of him.

Roman waits a few painful moments after the doctor leaves before speaking.

"You are my best fighter since Reaper."

His praise, if that's what it really is, comes unexpected. The stoic, colorless timbre of his words keeps me on guard as I wait for his censure.

"That's what everyone believes," he adds. "I wasn't convinced myself until tonight. Don't disappoint me like he did."

A small smile touches the corner of his mouth, but it's gone as fast as I can blink. My blood goes cold as adrenaline and terror combine to create paralysis. Earning something other than bored, unimpressed looks from Roman usually means I've failed him in some way. It means more training or discipline. For other boys unluckier than me, it means something far worse. When emotion breaks through his stone-faced mask, it means there will be a vacant room in the morning and one less fighter. Still, even a hint of emotion on his face is dangerous. Worst yet is his warning. I'll never forget what happened to Reaper.

Reaper died trying to break out of the Colosseum. He thought he was strong enough to stand up to Roman. He thought he could encourage the others to join. I remember wanting to believe him. I hadn't been at the

Colosseum long, and I still believed if I fought hard enough, I could somehow escape and make it back home. I thought Reaper was my answer. Roman shot those hopes down when he killed Reaper, every inch of his body covered in bullets. My aching hands go numb from gripping the sides of my bed.

I try to push the memories away and mirror Roman's stony look as his eyes search my face. His next words are as careful as his expression.

"You broke my rules. Foolish of you, but noble. And while I'm glad your survival instinct hasn't turned you into a complete animal, never disobey me again."

I manage to nod, but I don't dare speak. The darkest hint of emotion gleams in his blue eyes, a storm brewing, ready to break at any moment. A strong energy electrifies the room, like static charging the air. I hold my breath, waiting for the moment to pass. There's no way to gauge his mood or his course of action, no way to prepare. There's nothing more deadly than uncertainty.

"It's time," Roman says, turning his back on me. The tension dissolves. The feeling returns in my hands. My muscles ache like I've already been in a fight. Forcing myself up, I stumble after him. For years, I've felt like a constant failure. I don't know what it really means to be a champion in Roman's eyes. I'm not sure I want to find out. But there are no other options for me. It's either fight or die.

CHAPTER THREE

THE CAGE IS SURROUNDED BY THE USUAL crowds. I block out the noise, preparing for a war. I'm used to fighting giants. The harder they hit, the harder they fall. It's an odd but powerful thing to absorb the pain and channel it into my own power. Every hit, every impact, energizes my otherwise broken body to defy the odds stacked against me. My habit of knocking out much larger opponents has earned me the cage name Slingshot, some biblical reference about a kid slaying a giant with a slingshot and the giant's own sword.

Tonight, I'll have to slay ten giants if the other boys and I will have a chance at survival.

I shuffle into the empty ring. My heart drums so loud and hard, it comes through my ears, deafening all other noise. I wait and watch as my opponent enters the ring. One by one, the other boys file in. They circle me. Most are pale and worn. Some are close to feral, twisted by desperate hunger and a primal need to survive, no matter the cost. There is one face I don't recognize: a blond boy my age, taking in the Colosseum for the first time. He's the new recruit. With no training and no idea what he's facing, there's no way he would've survived a fight tonight.

I hesitate when the bell sounds, signifying the fight has begun. There's no sign of my usual competitor. My eyes search for Roman in the crowd. His brow arches just a fraction, and he nods once, motioning to the other boys. I look at them. They inch closer to me.

Nolan takes the lead, looming over me. "Sorry, Oliver."

He's taller and sturdier than my wiry frame. As sluggish as he moves, he delivers a powerful punch to my jaw. I draw in the pain as I stumble back.

"What are you doing?"

Nolan gestures at Roman. "The guy that beats you gets to go home. Our *real* home."

He swings at me again.

I duck. "And if you don't win?"

"Then it's no different than any other day."

He lunges at me. I sidestep him and push him away. Nolan's wrong. Nothing will ever be the same. Roman is testing us. He won't let any of them go, at least not in the way they expect. There will be another vacant cell. One less fighter. If I lose, someone will die, and the rest of us will starve.

"We'll rush him together. We're stronger together," Nolan says over the noise, but the others don't seem so sure.

Emery is taller than me too, but willowy in frame. He can barely stand. His back is hunched, and his drawn fists are weak. I can see the definition of his ribs outlined against his skin. He hasn't eaten in weeks.

"We can't all beat him. Roman's only

sending one of us home," Charlie says, shoving at Nolan.

Sighing, I aim for Emery first. All it takes is one punch. He falls to the floor, too weak to withstand the impact. He doesn't lose consciousness, but he doesn't have the strength to get back up.

Charlie charges at me. He's lean with big, powerful feet. I insert my foot between his and quickly sidestep as he loses his balance, tumbling forward. Dawson is one of the thicker guys, but even he's lost muscle tone. He runs at me with his head down. I take a step and meet resistance when Emery grips my heel from the ground level. I step on his other hand, and he releases his weak grip, but not before Dawson tackles me to the ground. My back cracks under the weight of his body. My nerves burn with fresh pain, and for a minute, I can't breathe. As Dawson holds me down with his elbow, the others circle us, assaulting me with punches and kicks. Dawson's larger frame shields me from some of the attack, but his elbow grinds into my shoulder, moving to my throat. With pressure on my upper body, my lower body is open for attack. I'm vulnerable. I'm losing. We're all going to starve.

No.

Something snaps. Instinct takes over, and with every pain-inducing hit, a wave of fury and power surges in a way I've never felt. I push up against the weight of Dawson's body, overpowering him until his back is to the ground. I straddle him and punch as fast and hard as I can until someone grabs me by the shoulders, dragging me off of his limp body. My body is wild with energy as I kick my legs up, flipping over. My feet meet someone's face, and I throw a blind punch at the next nearest body. The air is electric. Adrenaline surges, even as I lose all focus and reason. As much as I want to stop, to beg them to stop, I know I can't stop fighting. Even though I'm making them bleed, even though we're hurting each other, I'm fighting for them. I have to win. If I win, we all win.

I fight until only the blond boy remains. He's the only one who hasn't charged or challenged me. He's been watching from the sidelines. Our eyes connect, and I realize he isn't as afraid as I first thought. He's smart, determined even, waiting for everyone else to wear down so he can be the one left standing. I wish I could let him win, but there's too much at stake. He runs at me. I run in the opposite direction, knowing he isn't aware of my signature finishing move. I kick against the cage fence and propel forward to deliver the final hit.

I look up too soon. A flash of honey hair and an ashen face, pale and strained, catches me off guard. I lose momentum, missing my target, but I catch my balance at the last minute. My fist hits the hard cement, and the floor fissures beneath us as pain explodes from my knuckles, resonating through the nerves in my hand.

The blond boy flies back from the impacting wave. He lands in a disheveled, unconscious heap. The Colosseum rumbles, and the cage shakes, leaving the rowdy crowd in a shell-shocked stupor. Eyes widen. Mouths drop. Silence follows the echo of my misaligned punch.

My eyes wander to the face that made me miss my mark. It isn't often women come to the Colosseum. It's even more rare to see a girl. She hides her long, braided hair under a hood, but her large eyes draw me in to the rest of her face. She looks more disgusted than afraid. Her eyes meet mine, but I look away, burying a nauseating discomfort.

As sudden as the silence fell, the crowds roar back to life. I scan the drunken, high, sweaty faces for Roman. It isn't long before I see him at the side of the cage. He isn't watching, but his eyes are on the girl. I realize she sees Roman too. He moves toward her, lacing through the crowd.

Dr. Holden opens the cage to check on the other boys. He doesn't shut it behind him. I look for the girl again, but she's gone, and Roman's attention is back on the cage. A small frown plays at the corner of his mouth. For once, I hope the subtle show of emotion means something good. I hope the girl got away.

Our eyes meet, and Roman's frown inverts into a small, crooked smile. I'm the last boy standing, but I don't feel like a champion. I feel like a fool. Somehow, Roman is the real winner tonight.

CHAPTER FOUR

S ATISFIED WITH HIMSELF, ROMAN EXITS the Colosseum, followed by some of his men who have cleared the cage of unconscious bodies. Dr. Holden puts a hand on my shoulder, prodding me forward to follow the morbid procession.

I fall in line, scanning the crowd one last time for the girl. I hope she made it out OK. I hope she never comes back.

"Hey!"

A voice cuts through the Colosseum's clamor of booze, drugs, and betting.

"I'm talking to you, with the fancy punch!"

Hope crashes and burns at the sound of the feminine voice.

The girl shoves her way through the crowd of men that has gathered because they're startled to see her. This isn't a place for a girl. As she approaches the cage, taking off her hood, the crowd's initial shock recedes. There's annoyance, but more dangerous is the gleam of hunger and interest.

I turn to face her, all while Dr. Holden tries to pull me forward. I pull away from him and walk toward the girl. She doesn't cower but stands straight. Her face is no longer pale but flushed with anger.

She goads the crowds. "He bullies a bunch of sick boys and you call that a show?"

I frown. "You shouldn't be here."

Her large eyes are honey colored, but defiance shines through their natural warmth.

"Neither should you or any of those boys."

The familiar charge of adrenaline and power still lingers in the air. I can feel it pulsing, dancing on the surface of my skin, only second to the mounting fear I feel for her.

Dr. Holden calls for me. I ignore him.

"Do you know what these guys could do to you? What they do to girls like you all the time?"

She closes the space between us and looks me in the eye, something grown men twice her age don't have the nerve to do. "They're no match for me, and neither are you."

Dr. Holden reaches for me again. "Roman won't like this. Come on, boy."

The girl's eyes flash. "Fight me!"

Her challenge is met with whistles and catcalls.

I frown. "Leave."

She locks eyes with me. "I'm not going anywhere until you fight me."

The girl is persistent and brave, but the underground is no place for her. Roman would break her.

"Go home."

Dr. Holden touches my shoulder. "Security will take care of her."

He pulls at my arm again as some of Roman's guys materialize from the crowd. They surround the girl.

"Let's go," Dr. Holden says.

I hesitate. "They're going to let her go, right?"

He sighs. "It's better if you don't ask any questions. You have enough to worry about."

I watch as one of Roman's guys makes a grab for her arm. She swats his hand away.

"Don't touch me!"

I relax when one of the men gestures to the exit as the crowds mellow and break apart. Their entertainment is over. There will be no more fighting tonight. I cast the girl one last look before turning to follow Dr. Holden. I've barely taken a step when a rush of pressure beats against my back. I draw in a breath at the unexpected sensation and turn back to the girl when I hear the scream.

One of Roman's guys is twenty feet from where I last saw him, sprawled unconscious on the ground. The girl grips another man's arm and twists it at an odd angle. There's a loud crunch when she applies an extra bit of pressure. More of Roman's guys come at her, but they seem to move in slow motion. The girl lets go of the man's arm to dodge and maneuver around the other guys.

The lingering crowds gather. Some try to assist Roman's men, while others watch. The men surround her. She smiles at the challenge. Launching at the nearest man, her feet come off the ground. She jump-kicks one man, propelling off of him and into the next guy. She flips off of him and lands on the shoulders of the man beside him. The man struggles to throw her off, but she wraps herself tightly around his neck and pushes downward, driving him to the ground. She smashes his head against the concrete. The remaining men surround her cautiously, reaching for their weapons.

The girl rolls off the man's back and stands in one fluid motion, but she doesn't see all the guns. She doesn't know she's locked in a trap. The one-girl pandemonium drowns out Dr. Holden's cautioning voice, and it's only when I've punched the nearest gun-toting man that I realize how much trouble I'm in. It's too late to care now. All the other men turn their guns on me.

Guns sound off. I wait for the pain, but it's not a bullet that hits me. The girl dives into me, knocking us both down. She recovers fast on her feet and pulls me up with her. Her hand touches mine, and something like static electricity buzzes across my skin. I shiver at the familiar charge stirring. It's the same sensation I get when I'm revved up in a fight.

"Are you crazy? You're going to get yourself killed!" I yell over the gunshots, just as I realize the world is functioning in two different speeds. We're running, but the guys and their guns are moving in slow motion.

More gunshots explode from a different direction, jarring me out of my stupor. The noise comes from the halls leading away from the Colosseum. The girl wipes sweat from her face and grins.

"I'd level an entire city to save my brother, but honey, I'm just the distraction."

I see her fist coming at me, but by then, it's too late.

CHAPTER FIVE

I WAKE UP READY TO FIGHT, BUT MY COOR-dination is off. My body is worn, and my reflexes are out of sync. I tumble out of an unfamiliar bed, tangled in sheets and soft blankets. The room is dark, but I can see enough to know I'm in unfamiliar territory. The floor underneath my fingers is wooden, not cement, there are no bars on the door, and the room is twice as large as my normal space.

I can count on one hand the times I've been knocked unconscious, though one time is too many. Aside from the pain and the bad taste helplessness leaves in my mouth, it stirs up bad memories. I was twelve when I lost my last fight.

The door swings open as I struggle with the sheets and blankets. My tired limbs feel almost useless. A vaguely familiar face materializes and peeks at me from the doorway. It's the girl from the Colosseum. She blindly gropes for the switch on the wall and light floods the room, much brighter than my usual space. She shakes her head at me before setting a plate on a small, round nightstand by the bed.

"Finally awake. You must be starving."

The smell of grease and spices makes my mouth water. Hunger pangs cause my stomach muscles more pain than the kicks and punches from last night's fight, but I try to keep my face blank and my head clear.

"What was that last night?" I ask.

My voice is hoarse, and despite the hungry salivation, my throat is dry.

She raises an eyebrow and chuckles. "Last night? You've been asleep for almost two straight days. Either I hit you a little harder than I thought, or you really needed the sleep." She stoops to help me off the ground and scrunches her button nose. "And now, you need a shower. Have you ever showered? Do they let you shower?"

I scoot away from her, making one last desperate attempt to untangle myself from the blankets and sheets. "You talk too much."

The words slip, and I brace myself. If Roman were here, I'd be punished for talking out of turn. That kind of offense is met with fists, and those fists and the lessons that come with them are hard to forget. The girl shrugs my comment off, but her honey eyes scan my face.

She frowns. "They really did a number on you, huh?" When I don't answer, she stands and gestures to the food. "You're safe here. Eat, please. No funny business. No tricks. It's just bacon, eggs, and waffles."

Waffles. I haven't had waffles since I was seven. The thought of waffles gives me the willpower I need to pick myself up off the floor when I really feel like crawling. The food looks like a work of art, like a picture from a menu, worst yet, like something from Mom's kitchen. My throat tightens when I notice the strawberries and whipped cream decorating the waffles.

"You don't like it?" the girl asks.

I don't trust myself to answer. Instead, I pick up the little plastic fork from the plate and stab the scrambled eggs. My hands shake at the anticipation of eating my first home-cooked meal in four years. Before I know it, the fork is on the floor, and I'm eating with my hands.

She leans against the nearest wall. Her eyes drop to the floor. "When I was in the crowd, I heard them call you Slingshot."

I nearly choke on a stray bit of bacon in my throat. "Don't call me that."

"What should I call you then?"

Oliver.

The other boys from the Colosseum use my name, and on rare occasions, Roman does too. But sharing the only part of me that's left of my old life feels a little too personal, especially with the girl who knocked me unconscious.

"My name's Ivy," she says, then motions for me to introduce myself. I shove the last bit of waffle in my mouth and chew slowly, savoring the last of a good meal gone too soon. When I don't answer, Ivy frowns. "You're welcome, by the way."

I frown back at her, wondering what I could possibly be thankful for.

She gives me a pointed stare. "I saved your life."

Ivy's tough, and she's got some nice tricks up her sleeve. I've never seen anyone as strong or as fast as her, but she's no match for Roman.

"How long did you say I've been out of it?"

She shrugs. "About a day or two."

"Roman will kill you."

She grunts. "I'd like to see him try."

My stomach cramps from eating too much too fast, but I fight back a grimace, glaring at her instead. "You didn't save anyone. You stole his best fighter and left a huge mess."

All the men who failed to secure the Colosseum are likely dead. Maybe even Dr. Holden. He was already on Roman's bad side.

All the gunshots we heard that night … I don't even want to think about the dead bodies lining the halls to our cells.

Ivy's smug look disappears. A flicker of uncertainty crosses her face before her features harden with determination. "I got you out of that nightmare."

"I didn't ask you to."

She balls her fists up at her sides. "You didn't have to."

Her words surprise me. It's not often someone does something just because.

"My brother's in there. He's the blond boy you fought. We need your help to get him out of there."

My stomach tightens. "Who's we? Like you and the cops?"

Her confidence makes me nervous because it's the first time in a long time I've allowed myself even a sliver of hope. Survival has been my main goal. I never considered freedom. I never thought it would be an option.

"Not exactly," she says carefully.

I shake my head. "Then you should get as far away from here as possible. Roman—"

"Is no match for us. You saw what I can do, what you can do. We can take him down together."

I shoulder past her to get to the door, but she steps in front of me. "We've got a source and some intel on the place, but you've been living there for years. You probably know the ins and outs of the place."

She couldn't be more wrong. Over the last four years, I trained, fought, and lived in the Colosseum fighting cage. Otherwise, I've been locked in a dark cell, bandaged, bruised, and bloody, waiting to do it all over again. It's a vicious reality.

"I can't help you."

Ivy doesn't budge. "What are you going to do then? Go back home to your mommy and daddy? Because you're right. Roman will come looking for you, and he'll find you. You won't be able to hide from him."

I don't know where I'm going. I haven't had the time to process that I'm not at the

Colosseum anymore. It doesn't seem real. Maybe because I haven't made it out of the bedroom. Suddenly, I'm just as hungry for fresh air and sunlight as I was for the food.

"Move," I tell her.

She backs up slowly from the door. I move quickly, opening the door and running down a set of stairs. My mind races, bombarding me with broken, disjointed thoughts and emotions.

Am I really free?

I make my way to the front door a few feet from the stairs, race to the exit on shaky legs, and throw the door open. There is no sunlight, but a gray, cloudy overcast. The air is warm, heavy with moisture. I stumble down the porch steps. My legs buckle, and I fall into the muddy lawn. A light sprinkle of cool rain falls against my skin. Something I used to take for granted feels like a miracle. I dig my fingers into the lawn, enjoying the feeling of the grass and dirt. It's been so long since I've been outside, too long since I've breathed fresh air.

"This is the guy?"

Fresh air forgotten, I snap into attention. Ivy stands on the porch. She's not alone. The guy who spoke jogs down the steps. He's a few inches taller than me and built like the boys back at the Colosseum. The only difference is he's healthy, much stronger, and well fed. He's muscled where I'm lean, and he's got a bright, quick light to his eyes that many of the others lack. I ball up my fist as he approaches me. He extends a hand, and I swing.

He ducks. "Whoa, man! I was just gonna shake your hand."

My reflexes move on instinct. I swipe his legs with my foot, and he trips. I catch his shirt as he falls and raise my fist to meet his face.

"Don't hurt him!"

The last girl, a petite blonde, races across the yard. She leaps at me like a cat. I brace myself, expecting to catch her, but when we collide, she knocks the wind out of me. I fly through the air from the force of the attack, and when I land, I skid across the lawn. The friction burns into my back. Rolling to my side, I struggle to stand even though every nerve and cell feel like they're on fire. The blonde is small but much more powerful than the boy she's protecting. A hit like that should be impossible, but here I am, in worse shape than I've ever been.

Ivy's face materializes over me. "Way to go, Roxanne."

My chest feels heavy. I can barely breathe from the pain shooting through me. I try to block out the memories, but the pain makes it difficult. I fight to stay alert, anything to block the flood of memories triggered by the girl's punch. Only one other person has managed that kind of damage.

Roman's voice whispers in my head as the rest of the world fades to black. *"Sleep is for the dead."*

CHAPTER SIX

WHEN I COME TO AGAIN, MY ENTIRE body feels as sturdy as Jell-O. I'm not on a soft bed this time but, rather, on a couch with three sets of eyes staring back at me. I force myself to sit up. The room tilts.

Ivy gives me a light shove in the chest. I fall back into a fluffed pillow. She rests her hand on my shoulder as if she thinks it's the only thing that will keep me down.

"Tristan, I need the water. Rox, the pain pills."

A bottled water and two tiny white pills appear in her hand. I turn my face to the couch, a brown-and-gray-striped monstrosity.

She nudges my shoulder. "Outside of a week's worth of sleep, these should help with the pain."

I grit my teeth. "I'm used to it."

What I'm not used to is the physical contact. I barely remember what it feels like to be touched by something other than a punch or a kick. Maybe that's the worst part about touch; I've learned to expect pain and unlearn the comfort it can bring. My muscles tense when she pats my shoulder, readying my reflexes to respond to the slightest wrong move. I turn back to find her eyes trained on me.

She removes her hand as if she knows what I've been thinking, but her voice isn't defensive or tense when she speaks. "We aren't going to hurt you."

"As long as you don't try to hurt us," Rox says, peeking from behind Ivy.

"Not helping," Ivy sing-songs through her teeth. Her eyes never leave my face. She looks at me the way a hiker might look at a mountain lion. I'd seen a documentary on big cats once when I was seven. Maintaining eye contact minimized the risk of death.

"I don't trust him," Rox says. "What if he snaps again?"

I look past Ivy. "Like you?"

For someone so small, Rox is powerful, but restless. Looking at her pace, chewing on her nails, it's hard to believe she tackled me. It's even harder to believe she knocked me unconscious. Roman would cringe if he knew I'd been bested by not one but two girls. Then again, he always says the strongest fighters are the unpredictable ones.

Rox takes a step toward me, but the big guy is there to hold her back. She's easily provoked. Not as unpredictable as I thought.

Ivy sighs, drawing my attention back to her. "Give us a minute."

Rox hesitates, but Tristan ushers her out of the room, handling her like she's a dangerous explosive. Maybe she is. Maybe I am too. She knows what I'm capable of because we're made of the same stuff. I don't need to know her story to know she's got scars on her skin and some that run deeper. I recognize the signs of another survivor, another fighter.

Ivy waits until the others are out of the room before she speaks again, but I cut her off.

"No."

She frowns. "I haven't asked you anything yet."

"You want me to help you get your brother out of the Colosseum."

She raises her chin and mocks my tone. "No."

A smug smile settles on Ivy's face when I take the water and pills from her.

I frown. "What do you want?"

Her smile wavers. "Sometimes I want to set the world on fire and start it all over again, but it doesn't work that way."

Ivy may have soft, brown eyes and a nice smile, but I'm convinced she could set the world on fire if she wanted to. I saw some of that anger back at the Colosseum. She took out a room full of armed men who were no strangers to violence and brutality.

"I need intel," she admits. "Our first efforts were an epic fail."

"Not completely," I say. If it wasn't for Ivy, I'd still be locked up in the Colosseum. "I'm sorry about your brother."

There's a flicker of gentle surprise before her face hardens with determination.

"We've been casing the Colosseum from the crowd, watching their operations from the outside, but we need more information if we're going to save my brother and everyone else."

I shake my head. "You're delusional. The last guy that stood up to Roman ended up getting taken out with the trash."

Roman made us watch what his guys did to Reaper's bullet-ravaged body. It was something I'll never forget, something that's kept me in check when nothing else has over the years. Even now, when I'm free from the Colosseum, it serves as a cautionary tale to dissuade any thought of retaliation against the man who's made my life a nightmare for the last four years.

"I'm not that guy," Ivy says, drawing me back into the present moment.

"You're right. He was a legendary fighter."

Ivy rolls her eyes. "I'll take your word for it, but that's not what I meant. I'm not stupid enough to walk in there alone. We work as a team."

"You guys are no match for an entire compound of armed guards and trained fighters."

She stands, and her face flushes. "It wouldn't be the first seedy underground we've taken down. We've already put a drug network and a prostitution ring out of business. We're just getting started."

Ivy's been reading too many comic books. That's the only explanation I have for why she's so reckless. Being a superhero vigilante sounds great until someone dies. Reaper's death had curbed lots of my heroic fantasies. My last fight at the Colosseum destroyed the rest of it. I'd stuck my neck out for the guys, and they turned on me. The way they'd fought me hurt in more ways than one, but I'm not mad at them. I understand their desperation.

The thought of being free, going home, and not having to fight anymore … I didn't leave the Colosseum on my own two feet, but I don't have the strength or the courage to walk back into that place.

"I'm not going back there."

Ivy sighs. "Just tell us what you know about the place. That's all we're asking."

As if sharing my personal trauma with a bunch of strangers is any easier. Then again, maybe I can scare them with all the details and talk them out of whatever stupidity they're planning. Agility and strength are nothing compared to what Roman has up his sleeves.

Ivy frowns. "I wish I could be polite about this, but we've already wasted enough time. My brother's in that place. I have to get him out of there."

I remember her brother. He nearly kept me up all night before that last fight, banging on the doors and swearing in the dark. He'd been the last guy standing in the ring the next night, calculating, watching while the rest of us were at each other's throats. There was a ferocity in his eyes that I hadn't seen in others. Some fighters liked to look strong. Her brother looked like he liked to fight.

"I think he'll last longer than the three of you."

Ivy's tough, but her connections are her biggest weakness. All Roman has to do is threaten her brother, and she'll probably fall apart. Tristan seems a little too nice and polished to do what it takes to put a monster like Roman down. And Rox? With a punch and an attitude like hers, Roman would take her out first. Out of the four of them, Ivy's brother has the best chance at survival.

"You don't understand," she says, her voice rising an octave higher. "Max isn't like us. He's tough, but—"

Rox burst into the room. Tristan stumbles behind her.

"It's been a minute," the blonde says. "Are you going to help us or not?"

"He's not going anywhere until he tells us what we want to know," Ivy says.

I'm on my feet before I realize it, standing inches apart from Ivy. "Is that a threat?"

She flinches but recovers with a smirk. "Looks like those pain pills are working."

My skin bristles. She may have knocked me out once, but it won't happen again. She had the element of surprise before. Now, I have the advantage.

"I told you we couldn't trust him!" Rox growls.

I see her move out of the corner of my eye. She swings at me. I dodge. Ivy doesn't. Rox hits her in the face, and she plummets to the ground, clutching her nose. The blonde shrieks and throws another punch. I grab her fist, twist her arm, and press down on the pressure point between her thumb and index finger. She screams, and her knees buckle.

Tristan moves faster, and he's much lighter on his feet than I calculated. He snatches Rox out of my grip and stands in front of her like a shield. With Rox out of the way, he lunges at me, but I've adapted to his speed. I parry around him and use an open palm to strike his temple. His hands raise to clutch his head, leaving open access for more places to attack. Heat radiates in my hand as I form a fist. The familiar wave of energy charges through my veins, and I swing.

"Stop!" Ivy screams.

I freeze, barely able to contain the inertia. "You caught me off guard once, but it won't happen again. You did some damage to the Colosseum the first time, but Roman will be ready for you next time. None of you will make it out alive."

CHAPTER SEVEN

STUNNED SILENCE GREETS ME, JUST like all my other fights. The only difference is no one's unconscious. Ivy presses down on her nose to stop it from bleeding, but her wide eyes never leave my face. Rox stands like she could leap back into action at any minute, but her face projects hesitance and uncertainty. Tristan shuffles to the couch, careful to keep his distance from me. He collapses on the couch and reaches for the pills. We all watch, silent and frozen, as he drinks my leftover water and swallows a few tablets. He shakes his head and salutes me with the water bottle.

"I am your new best friend, OK? I don't ever want to get on your bad side."

Ivy wipes the blood from her nose with the back of her hand. "OK, K.O., I'll admit you have some moves."

Moves are for dancers. I'm the Colosseum's champion. I've got skills.

"K.O.?" Tristan echoes.

She snorts. "Yeah. He gives a punch as good as he takes it."

Rox grimaces. "That's a better name than Slingshot."

"What's your real name, though?" Tristan wonders.

Rox circles me, no longer hostile but curious. "Can you teach me that thing you did to my hand? After you take a shower and change clothes, I mean. You smell."

The closer she gets and the more she talks, the more on edge I feel. We don't do a lot of socializing at the Colosseum. When we aren't training or fighting, our living space is small, dark, and quiet. I'm not used to the space, the light, the noise. It hadn't hit me before, but as Rox reaches out to pick at my hair, all the sensations seem to amplify. My body tenses, and I step back to avoid her touch. It takes significant effort not to swat her hand.

My stomach growls. Tristan perks up at the noise. "You're hungry? Me too. I'll go make some bacon sandwiches. You like gouda?"

"Gouda?" I repeat, trying to focus on something, anything.

He stares at me expectantly. "Gouda cheese."

Rox taps me. I flinch, but she doesn't notice. "What size do you wear? We've got to take you shopping."

I open my mouth, not sure who I should respond to first: the nitpicking blonde inspecting my clothes or the guy asking a thousand questions in the space of a few seconds. Tristan doesn't give me a chance to respond. He rambles on about sourdough bread and hickory bacon, raving about what makes the perfect bacon sandwich.

Rox eyes my feet, shaking her head. "I don't know how they expected you to fight in those atrocities."

There are holes and rips in my black tee and pants, but my clothes are comfortable and functional. Dried mud cakes the sides and bottom of my boots. The shoestrings are frayed, and the black color has turned into a dusted gray. But my boots are sturdy and comfortable on my feet. I frown at her. I think I liked her better when she didn't like me. She didn't talk so much.

Tristan whistles and waves his hands to get my attention. "K.O.? Can we really call you that? You want your bread toasted?"

I just bested all three of them in a fight and told them they're going to die. Now, they're giving fashion advice and offering me food. I'm not an expert on normal, but I have the odd impression this bunch is just as screwed up as I am. The fact that they're organizing a raid on the Colosseum should've been my first clue. I massage my temples to avoid an oncoming headache.

Rox snaps her fingers in my face. "Hey, how do you feel about a haircut?"

My hair is long, but I keep it tied up out

of my face. I haven't thought much about it or anything else. Style isn't high on a fighter's list of priorities at the Colosseum.

"Guys! Focus!" Ivy snaps. "Max is counting on us."

I rub my face. "Didn't you hear anything I said? If you go back to the Colosseum, you're dead."

"If we don't go, Max is dead," she counters.

Tristan raises his hand. "I'm all for not dying."

Ivy glares at him. "We can't just abandon Max."

Tristan frowns. "I didn't say that. I just know we can't help anybody if we're dead."

She turns her glare on me. "We can't leave him there. You know he won't survive. I have to do something."

Tristan's frown deepens, and Rox shuffles her feet.

Everyone is quiet long enough for me to process their words. I stare at Ivy's panicked face. Swollen nose aside, her eyes are bright with fear.

"When you said he wasn't like you, what did you mean?"

"Max is tough, but he's just a regular guy."

"Then he's probably already dead, and you're risking your life for nothing," I say, though I'm not as sure as I sound.

Roman doesn't enlist just *anybody* in the Colosseum. If he took her brother, there must be something to him. There *is* something to him. There has to be. I don't want to care. I want to live. I want to be free. I'm tired of fighting, but Roman's mantra is drilled into my conscience. *"Rest is for the weak."*

I've spent four years enduring pain and fighting nonstop for the enjoyment of others at my own expense. I've been fighting to earn some semblance of security and approval from a monster. The night he finally acknowledged everything I worked so hard to win, Ivy showed up. He called me his champion, and he warned me not to fail him like Reaper. I'm not his champion anymore, and if I step one toe back into the Colosseum, I'm dead too.

"Coward. Weak. Worthless." Roman's voice continues to echo in my head.

As hard as it is to believe, Ivy got me out of that cycle. The least I can do is give her the same chance to save her brother. Maybe they can even give the other boys what I couldn't: a real, fighting chance. Not just to survive another day or another week, but a chance to really live. I'll be weak if it means I can sleep in peace. I'll be a coward if it means I can finally live a normal life. But I refuse to be worthless.

I grit my teeth. "I'll take that shower and that bacon gouda with the sourdough. Then, I'll tell you what you want to know."

CHAPTER EIGHT

I WAS TEN WHEN I REALIZED I WASN'T AN average kid. Some boys at school were picking on me, and I decided to fight back. One punch put one of my tormentors in the hospital. He was in a coma for a week. His parents pressed charges, and I was expelled from school and almost went to juvie. My mom couldn't understand how her brilliant little scholar could be so violent. We talked about it in the grocery store the day I was abducted.

"No one likes a bully."

Those were the last words she ever said to me. She'd been so busy talking at me that I never had the chance to tell her what led up to that moment. I was still in shock myself. I'd gone from being a slip of a kid to the scariest thing on the playground. I went from being the kid everyone picked on to the kid everyone whispered about and avoided. I walked the empty shopping cart slowly across the parking lot so she wouldn't see me cry. I'd even thought about running away.

"We all have our trauma." Ivy's voice jars me out of the painful memories, and for a second, I wonder if she can read my mind. But that's impossible. Maybe about as impossible as what we're able to do. "We all have our stories, but somehow, our strength, our speed, and everything else showed up when we needed it most. The survival instinct kicks in. Adrenaline spikes off the charts and jump-starts our extras."

Those extras hadn't kicked in when I really needed them. I'd fought with everything I had to get back to Mom in that grocery store parking lot, then several times more to escape the Colosseum. When Reaper died, I gave up on freedom and settled for survival.

"Our informant calls us Errants. He says that when our survival instinct is triggered and our Errant abilities kick in, it gives off a signal. Kinda like …"

Her voice trails off as she searches for the right word.

"Static?" I ask.

Her face brightens. "Yeah. That's it."

I pull at my oversized jogging pants for the tenth time as everyone huddles around the couch. The bacon sandwich with the weird cheese sits heavy on my stomach. Ivy's eyes search my expression. I keep my face as impartial as I can. Roman's voice is always in my head. *You're only as vulnerable or as strong as what you show. Unpredictability is strength.*

When I first came to the Colosseum, Roman let all the new recruits know we hadn't been taken by accident. We'd been chosen to serve a greater purpose. He didn't take us from our homes and our families to traffic us, but to train us. We belonged to him. We were his gladiators, his *fleet*. I still remember him stooping to meet me at eye level. It was the only other time I'd seen him smile. *"I've had my eye on you for some time."*

I'd never thought much about it before, but now, I wondered. Maybe he first noticed me through the small-town gossip, or the news alerted him of the "small kid who snapped and put his classmate in a coma." But if what Ivy says is true, he could have easily detected my powers. If I use my hyper-strength or agility, there's a chance he can find me again, any of us.

I shake my head, trying to empty my mind of the terrifying possibility, but the more I try, the more it settles in and the more dread creeps in.

"Who is this contact? Are you sure you can trust him?"

She shrugs. "He calls himself John Doe. Max and I were searching for answers on the Internet when he hacked our systems and introduced himself. We haven't seen his face, and he used a voice synthesizer when we spoke directly, but he hasn't steered us wrong so far."

I lean back against the couch, the nausea building.

"What is it?" Ivy asks.

I do my best to keep my tone flat and emotionless. "If our abilities give off a signal, how far does the signal go? How strong is it?"

"Depends on the amount of power. Small bursts require a closer range. But something like the Colosseum gives massive waves of it. It got John's attention. He's the one who asked us to check it out," she answers.

"Are all the boys at the Colosseum Errants like us?" Tristan asks.

"I think he chooses members of the fleet specifically because we have the ability. Our training is designed to push us to the limits, to trigger our powers. No one without those powers lasts long."

Ivy pales. Rox grips her limp hand and eyes Tristan. Ivy, unaware of Rox's attempt to comfort her, pulls away and leans forward.

"What kind of training?"

Roman's words might as well be tattooed on my skin. "He has a saying that he beat into us until it was second nature. 'Rest is for the weak. Sleep is for the dead. Fight or die. Win or starve.' It's as simple as that."

"With that attitude, he won't have much of a fleet," Tristan mutters.

"It's not about the numbers for him. He'd rather have one perfect soldier than one hundred mediocre ones."

Rox crosses her arms. "What's he building an army for? World domination or something?"

Ivy jumps up. "I don't care why he's doing this. I want my brother back, and I'm not waiting another day."

"Max might not be an Errant, but he's tough, stubborn, and he loves a good fight. He's pretty much you without the hair," Tristan says, earning a smile from Ivy.

"This guy's going down. I know we barely got out of there last time, but there's no way those other boys want to stay there. They'll stand with us, right?" Rox asks.

Ivy shakes her head. "Last guy that tried to start a rebellion was gunned down."

"Maybe we should go to the cops or FBI and let them handle this one," Tristan suggests.

"Then we'll all end up being lab experiments of the government!" Rox says.

Tristan sighs. "You've been watching too many superhero movies."

Rox swings at him. He ducks and chuckles. Watching them play around in the middle of planning a rescue mission makes me realize how much I've missed. We don't play at the Colosseum. We don't joke. Everything is a matter of life and death. There's no middle ground. There's no rest. By now, Roman knows Ivy and the others are coming for Max. He'll use it to his advantage. He's smarter, stronger, and has way more discipline than them. If they're smart, they'll cut their losses and leave the city before he tracks them down too.

What if he already has? The thought crosses my mind, causing the hairs on my arm to rise. I've been away from the Colosseum for just a few days, but we've been using our powers loosely, sitting idly like we don't have a care in the world. I shouldn't be here.

I stand up, tightening the pants Tristan loaned me as much as I can. "I'm not staying here. You won't either if you know what's good for you."

"What is it?" Ivy asks, but she freezes. Her eyes widen. She knows. She feels it, and so do the others. There's a subtle hint of static in the air. It's light at first, but then it comes in waves until it overwhelms everything around us.

We've been debating about how to get back into the Colosseum, how to get to Roman. But he's brought the fight to us.

CHAPTER NINE

AN OVERWHELMING SENSE OF FEAR AND desperation mutes all conscious reasoning. Instinct kicks in. I race for the door, nearly taking it off its hinges so I can get out. A boy stands on the porch. His blond hair is dirty. Cuts and bruises line his face. I can tell there are more injuries by the hunched way he stands. Recognition sparks light in otherwise tired eyes. It's Roman's newest recruit, the last boy I fought in the room.

"Max!"

Ivy rushes past me to throw her arms around her brother. He winces at the impact but slowly, painfully, returns her embrace.

The others gather around the door, joining the siblings in their reunion, but Max's eyes find mine.

"Where are they?"

He looks up to the roof just as two figures drop down beside him. Nolan steps forward.

"Hello, Oliver."

Ivy, Tristan, and Rox pull away from Max, moving back toward me.

Tristan winces. "Oliver? *That's* your name?"

Rox nudges him with her elbow. He yelps.

Dawson stands on the other side of Max. He spits, and the liquid lands at Rox's feet.

She glares at him. "That was rude." She lunges forward, but Tristan holds her back.

Nolan's lip curls. "You left us. Found new friends."

"I didn't leave you, but I'm not going back."

Ivy reaches for her brother. "Max, get inside."

He backs away from her as the other two advance forward.

Dawson cracks his knuckles. "A lot's changed since you were gone."

Tristan snorts. "It was only a few days. Not like he was gone a year."

Dawson strikes quick, sucker punching Tristan in the face. He's out cold before he hits the ground. Rox pounces at Dawson. Her strength defies the difference in their forms as her small frame sends him flying backward through the air. She lands on top of him, but he recovers quickly, rising up to pin her down. She pushes her elbow into his windpipe to disable him before securing him in a headlock. She wrestles him to the ground, but not without effort.

Nolan watches Rox with detached interest before turning his full attention to me. "She'll make a nice addition to the Fleet."

Ivy steps in front of me. "She's not going anywhere with you. None of us are."

Nolan smirks. "You're the one-woman army Roman's so interested in getting his hands on. Ivy, is it? Roman's got a proposition for you. You and your little team join the Fleet willingly, and he'll let you all live. Almost all of you." His eyes roam everywhere but Ivy's face before he looks at me again. "You're no longer needed or wanted."

Ivy rakes a hand through her hair and closes the distance between her and Nolan. She runs her fingers across his shoulder before raising her knee, striking him in the groin. When he curls in from the impact, she head-butts him. He staggers backward, one hand to his pants, the other to his head.

"That's my answer. Max, get in the house!"

Her brother hasn't moved or spoken since they showed up. He stands, almost shell-shocked, detached and frozen. Roman can have that impact on a person.

Nolan straightens quickly from Ivy's assault. He rubs his head and sighs. "Don't make this hard, Oliver. You know what happens if you don't come with us."

"You don't have to do what he says," Ivy says. "We can fight him together."

Nolan ignores her, focusing on me now. "When you disappeared ... he took it out on us.

Dr. Holden and some of the guys didn't survive. They were too weak to defend themselves. If I don't bring you back, *all* of you, we're all dead. You can't get away from him. None of us can."

"Why doesn't he come get us himself?" Ivy asks, voicing the question running through my own mind.

Nolan is no match for me, especially with Ivy and Rox's help. Roman knows that too.

Nolan glares at me. "You were always feeding us your scraps like you were doing something that mattered, like you were some kind of hero. This is your chance to really prove it. Tonight, you'll fight him."

I feel a sharp sting in my neck just as Ivy cries out. I pull a small, needled dart out as Nolan backs off the porch and limps down the lawn. The tranquilizer races through my system faster than any narcotic I've ever taken for pain. My limbs are numb before I hit the ground, but I fight to stay conscious. That's when I notice Rox. She's knocked out cold next to a recovering Dawson. The same dart sticks out from her neck.

Nolan pats Max's back. "Good job, man."

Max winces from the physical contact. Nolan kicks Dawson in the side. "Get up. We've got bodies to carry."

<hr>

The strong wave of Errant power jolts me out of unconsciousness. Though I'm still disoriented from the heavy tranquilizer, it doesn't take me long to recognize the small space. The familiar musty scent of the molded cell stings my nose. My two seconds of freedom might as well have been a dream, but I miss the fresh air already.

An unfamiliar voice greets me in the dark. "Finally awake."

I sit up too fast. "Who's there?"

Hot bile burns the back of my throat.

"Your replacement."

Cold chills course through me. I shake it off as best as I can. The light snaps on, and though it's dim, my eyes sting.

I use my hand to shield my eyes as Max strides in. "You're not an Errant."

He leans against the wall, spinning something in his hand. "True, but I'm a great negotiator."

"You told Roman about your sister."

He shrugs. "I told him two truths and a lie."

If Max's answers for Roman were half as frustrating as they are for me, it's no wonder he's in such bad shape.

"The guy's obsessed with building an elite team of fighters. He felt Ivy and my friends using their extras when they took down the neighboring drug and prostitution rings. He was disappointed to know he'd grabbed the wrong kid. So in between begging him not to kill me and getting the crap beat out of me, I asked him what he needed fighters for. He started monologuing about 'an old enemy and a coming war.' So, I recommended Ivy, Tristan, and Rox so he wouldn't kill us. It's not like he has to train them. They're already taking down entire underground networks."

"And where does that leave the rest of the guys?" I ask.

He approaches me slowly, leaving the door wide open behind him. "I think Roman's ready to kill them and sell their body parts on the black market."

Anger disintegrates the cold chills, but I work to keep my face neutral. "And that doesn't bother you?"

Something flashes in his hand again, but it's gone before I can register what it is.

"It's the opposite of OK. I like the guys, but there's nothing I can do to help them. But you can."

"You're the one who suggested I fight him?"

Max grins. "It's genius but too melodramatic for me. That was all him." His jaw slackens, and his smile fades just as soon as it came. His lips tremble, and he covers his mouth with his hands. "H-he was really angry when he found out you were gone. He kinda lost it, a-and he killed that doctor, all his security detail, a-and half of the other boys. T-there was nothing anyone could do. I-I couldn't …" Max's voice cracks. He swallows hard before attempting to pull himself together. "You were his champion fighter. No one else can take you down but him. And no one has a better shot of destroying that monster than you."

I don't have to imagine the horror. I've lived it. I've seen the violence Roman is capable of on many occasions. The bodies dragged out like trash. Half-broken shells of boys discarded while they were still breathing. The blood, the screams …

"Did the other guys tell you about—"

Max nods. "Reaper? Yeah."

"Then you know I can't win this fight. Reaper was the best fighter I've ever seen, and he didn't stand a chance."

Max frowns at me. "You did hear the part where I told you he killed all the guys with guns, right? He can't send his firing squad after you if they're all dead."

Life is one big slice of cruel irony.

Max shrugs. "They call you Slingshot for a reason around these parts, right? You slay all the giants."

"No one that matters calls me that," I snap.

He raises his hands and slowly lowers

himself to sit next to me on the bed. He grimaces. "Oliver, Ollie? I can call you that, right?"

I nod. After the beating he took, he's pretty much an official member of the Colosseum.

"I'll tell you something my mom said to me and Ivy before she skipped town and left us with our crazy dad. 'As long as we have each other, we'll be just fine.'"

CHAPTER TEN

THERE ARE NO SCREAMING CROWDS TO-night, just solemn faces. I enter the cage, my heart hammering mercilessly in my chest with each step. I've never felt so hopeless or alone.

Max leans his back against the wire of the cage. He turns his head slightly, whispering loudly through his teeth. "No pressure or any-thing. Just remember, if you die, we're pretty much all done for."

There are ten of us—Ivy, Tristan, Rox, Max, Nolan, Dawson, Emery, and just a few other fa-miliar faces. The stark decline in our numbers sharpens my fear and clouds my focus.

I feel Roman coming before I see him. Waves of static overwhelm the air. It's hard to breathe, almost as if I'm drowning. He enters the cage, slamming the door behind him. His usual suit and tie are gone, replaced with black joggers and boots identical to my own. His chest is well toned, defined, and covered in scars. Just like mine.

I force myself to face him, mirroring his face and posture like he taught me. I iron out every emotion, matching his apathetic mask. I'm vibrating with fear. The fear is strong, very strong, but there's power underneath that terror, and that power is greater. It has to be. I channel that fear, fueling the well of power within me. It builds like a small fire, radiating a warmth that spreads tentatively through my veins. Where his energy is oppressive and heavy, I'm just warming up. I'm no match for him, but I'm not powerless. *"Unpredictability is strength."*

He opens his arms wide and motions me forward, giving me permission to make the first attack. He looks wide open and vulnerable, but I know better. He's testing me, trying to gauge my strengths, my weaknesses. I open my arms, mimicking him, baiting him just as he did me.

His mask breaks into a slow, knowing smile. "I trained you well." I make the mistake of blinking. Before I know it, he rushes me, jabbing my middle with an uppercut. I fold into his fist as my insides explode into crippling pain. The pain radiates from my abdomen up through my throat, filling my mouth with the coppery taste of blood. He grabs my hair. "Which is why you're such a disappointment."

Staring into his wild eyes, I soak up his hatred. Maybe he's not in control like I thought.

I smile. "That's the nicest thing you've ever said to me."

He growls, using one hand to grab my throat. He squeezes, and I feel my eyes bulge. My head swells, expanding as I gasp for air even as my airways constrict. Blindly, I feel for his hands, vainly, weakly trying to free myself from his grip. He picks me up by the throat and slams me into the ground. Black floaters make it difficult to see.

"Fight me or die," Roman says.

I spit out a mouthful of blood. His mantra no longer makes sense. Even if I fight, I'm going to die tonight.

"I'm tired of fighting."

I'm not even sure if I can stand.

"Rest is for the weak," he counters.

I laugh. "Sleep sounds good. Get on with it."

I lay flat on my back and spread. I'm not sure I can move, even if I wanted to. My body is so tired, and it hurts so much that I feel everything and nothing all at once. I should have listened to Dr. Holden. I should've kept my head down and settled for survival. Maybe he and the other boys would still be alive if I had. Standing up to bullies never got me anything but trouble, and now, it's going to get me killed. Only, I'm not standing up to Roman. I'm giving up. A nagging buzz of electricity snakes its way through my veins, power that I don't have the strength or courage to use.

Max's words interrupt my thoughts. *"No one else can take you down but him. And no one has a better shot of destroying that monster than you."*

Roman looms over me. He raises a foot to smash in my face. I feel the force of the blow well before it drops.

"They call you Slingshot for a reason around these parts, right? You slay all the giants."

But the force of his foot is met by resistance. Instinct kicks in as my conscious mind and rationale retreat, surrendering to the power that's been waiting to break out. I feel the pushback as Roman pushes his boot down on my hand. I manage to move my face just as he smashes my hand into the ground. The pain sends a shockwave through me, but the power in me emits a stronger wave. A surge of energy shoots through me, coupled with strength like I've never known before. It numbs every pain and energizes the most tired parts of me. I beat at Roman's leg with my free hand, and when that doesn't work, I bite at his ankle. His leg buckles, and he falls on one knee. I tear my hand from under his weight, cradling it to my chest as I scramble to my feet. Roman has already recovered from my insubstantial defense.

I rush to the far side of the cage, push off the side, and propel forward. Roman grabs me out of midair and slams me into the nearest side of the cage before jabbing into my already-injured abdomen over and over. I step on his foot and push into him with my elbow to take him off balance. He pushes back until he rams me up against the side of the cage, pushing his elbow into my throat. I reach wildly for whatever I can get my hands on, managing to claw at his eyes. He recoils, moving to protect his eyes. I rush him, bombarding his temples with as many hits as I can get. He moves to cover his head, but I don't let up. I aim harder, faster, with as much energy as I can muster.

Blood covers my fists as I hit beyond Roman's hands and arms, reaching his face. I don't stop until he's swaying on his knees. His eyes roll back to the whites. I deliver one last blow, channeling all my anger, rage, and fear into the hit. He collapses to the ground in one large heap. But I don't stop beating into him until Ivy's there, prying me off of him.

"Stop, you got him. You did it," she says.

With the immediate threat subdued, my Errant abilities lift. The pain from my injuries comes roaring back to life. My legs give out on me, but Ivy braces me. Tristan supports me from the other side, and they usher me slowly out the cage.

"You should've let me kill him."

Nolan and the others gather around me, slowly, tentatively, as if they're afraid.

"You had me worried for a minute. I thought I might have to jump-start your heart or something," Max says, materializing a syringe.

Ivy snatches it from him. "What is that? Where'd you get it from?"

Max takes it back from her. "It's adrenaline. I found it in the late doctor's stuff and thought it might be handy."

"What are we going to do with Roman now?" Nolan asks. "We can't just let him walk free."

We all look back to the cage where his body should be. A wave of energy surges, and we all tense as Roman materializes. He moves so fast; my tired eyes can't work fast enough to keep up with him. It isn't until his swollen, bloodied face is inches from mine that I realize I haven't beaten him at all. I can't summon any more strength. I can barely stand, but Roman is still pulling on his Errant abilities, a seasoned fighter with much more stamina. He throws himself at me, tearing me away from my friends, his hands grasping for my throat. A sharp slice through the air halts his moves. I look up to see the syringe Max was holding now embedded in his left eye. His eyes grow large, and his mouth stretches wide, but no sound comes out. He doesn't even have time to pull the syringe out before he collapses, dead, taken out by a Non-Errant with a shot of adrenaline. His body was already in overdrive from using his power. The added adrenaline was too much on his heart. We were finally free.

EPILOGUE

WE SIT ON A FIRE ESCAPE ADJACENT TO a modest apartment in New Jersey, staring into the window. I tell Savannah the last few details of my time in Kansas. How we raided the Colosseum for weapons, supplies, money, anything we could use to start a new life. The money from the Colosseum and other underground networks Ivy and the other Errants collected was used to fund what would become a new Fleet.

Many of us, myself included, didn't know where our birth families were or didn't feel like we could return to them. We were different, damaged. Roman had left a stain on our souls. He'd held us captive for years, training us for a war we didn't understand, a war we never thought we'd see. Our powers attracted others like us, and within just a year's time, we built a new life and a new family. We met our John Doe a few years later. He was a baby-faced teen with zits and a crackly voice, but we called him Geezer.

Savannah laughs. "Geezer was giving Max and Ivy intel when he was ten?"

I smile.

Life was one big slice of cruel irony.

Roman's enemy was real. The Immortals could sense our power too, and when they came for us, we weren't ready. A lot of people died, including Nolan and Ivy. Losing Ivy is what finally triggered Max's Errant abilities, and it tore us apart. Max had her same reckless, fighting spirit, and with abilities, he only got worse. Tristan, Rox, Geezer, and I decided to come to New York. We left Max behind, but he eventually followed.

"What is this place?" Savannah wonders, staring at the modest apartment.

The family that lives inside is asleep now, all except one. A light comes on in one of the two bedrooms, and a small child peeks out through the window.

I lean close to whisper. "Geezer suggested the New York area because he knew it would be close to my birth family. He found them for me."

Savannah's eyes widen. "How did they take it the first time you showed up at their door?"

I look away from her, back to the little boy playing with a toy train. "They don't know I'm here. They can't know about me. Not with the Immortals after us."

She's quiet for a moment. I know she's thinking about her own mom.

"So you just sit out here and watch them?"

"You think it's creepy?"

She bites her lip. "No. Just sad. I'm sure they miss you."

We watch the little boy a little while longer

until he turns out his light again. Savannah yawns and rests her head on my shoulder again. I know it's because she's exhausted, but I'm starting to look forward to moments like this.

"We'll beat the hunters," she whispers.

I rest my head gently on hers as she snuggles closer. "I know."

There's a world hidden in the folds of everyday life. I slipped through those cracks, and though I've fought with everything in me to escape, I keep getting pulled back down. I've been drafted into a war I never knew existed, but I've been slaying giants for a while now. Being an Errant comes with its perks, but agility and strength are not my greatest weapons. I'm finding that my greatest power comes from the fact that I'm not as alone as I once thought.

Acknowledgements

To my family and friends, thank you for your love, support, and patience. Thank you for your constant encouragement, for letting me read and ramble on about all my bookish ideas. I'm grateful for you and love you all so much.

Thank you to everyone who helped put this work together: to my beta readers and ARC reviewers, to Make Your Mark Publishing Solutions and Raw Design Studios.

To the Greatest Author & Creator. With God, all things are possible.

About the Author

Montrez is a fantasy and science fiction author who lives in the moody Midwest with her husband and two sons. She loves writing about extraordinary worlds hidden in the folds of ordinary places and everyday life.

Don't be a stranger! Join the Novel Creature Community at www.authormontrez.com for the latest updates and exciting giveaways.

Thank you for reading *Knockout*
If you've enjoyed this book, please help
spread the word by leaving an online review.

KEEP IN TOUCH WITH MONTREZ

Website: www. authormontrez.com
Facebook: montrezstories
Instagram: @montrezwrites
Twitter: @montrezwrites

www.ingramcontent.com/pod-product-compliance
Lightning Source LLC
Chambersburg PA
CBHW021204110726

47900CB00002B/732